THE HAUNTED LAKE

P.J. LYNCH

WALKER BOOKS
AND SUBSIDIARIES

LONDON • BOSTON • SYDNEY • AUCKLAND

No one but old Reuben and his son, Jacob, fished Lake Spetzia. People said it was haunted.

Before there was a lake, Spetzia was the name of the village that had been there, and of the river that ran through it, but the water company had dammed the river, flooding the valley and the village to make a reservoir of clean water for the town below the mountains. Most of the villagers were given new houses in the big town, but not Jacob and his father. Their house was safe on the hill. Reuben wouldn't leave anyway, because Jacob's mother, Celia, was buried in the cemetery below the lake.

Now all that could be seen of their village was the old clock tower.

Reuben had been a farmer, but now most of his fields were underwater, so he and Jacob became fishermen. Young Jacob quickly learned where the rooftops came close to the surface, and he guided his boat skillfully between them. It was there that the biggest fish always swam.

Reuben and Jacob worked hard fishing the lake. In the evenings, they gutted and hung their catch in the smokehouse, and on Fridays they took their fish to the market in town.

Every week a mother and her young daughter, Ellen, bought their fish. While her mother paid for the fish, Ellen whispered to Jacob, "You're the fishers from the haunted lake, aren't you?"

"Shush, Ellen!" her mother scolded.

But Reuben recognized the woman from the old days at Spetzia and smiled at the young girl, inviting them to come to the lake.

That Sunday, Ellen and her mother visited the lake. Jacob and his father took them out in their boat. Ellen thought it was funny how the clock tower stuck out of the lake, but her mother cried when the boat glided above her old house, almost close enough for her to touch the chimney.

Ellen and her mother visited a few more times, and then, when she was older, Ellen came by herself.

She swam close to the shore and played with the animals. While Jacob and his father were out on the lake, she cooked fish soup and boiled potatoes for supper. When it was ready, she rang a handbell to call Jacob and his father home.

Later, Jacob taught Ellen to sail and to fish. One day when they were fishing together, Ellen declared that she would marry Jacob.

"I'm too old for you, lass," he said. "You are fourteen, and I'm an old man of nineteen."

But Ellen had set her heart on Jacob.

Folks from the big town below told Ellen, "Stay away. There are ghosts in that lake. The bell in the tower rings whenever another poor soul is going to join them down below."

"Nonsense," said Ellen. "That's just me ringing the handbell for the men's dinners."

But even she was uneasy when Jacob began to fish in the dark evenings. There were dangerous currents in the lake, and in winter the weather could turn bad very quickly.

"Don't worry," said Jacob. "No one knows that lake like me. I know how to get the big fish to come out from their hiding places among the old houses. I reckon I'll catch a perch or two tonight, lass, and I'll need to catch twice as many if I am ever to marry."

Ellen blushed and Jacob splashed her as he pushed his boat away from the small dock.

"I didn't say I was going to marry you, though, did I?" He laughed. "Don't you know I have a princess waiting for me out in the tower? Rapunzel ... Rapunzel, I'm coming."

Jacob never missed a day of fishing, and the three of them worked hard gutting and smoking and salting the fish. So much fish that Jacob bought a bigger cart to haul it all to market.

Every day they spent together, Jacob and Ellen grew closer and their love grew stronger.

For his twenty-first birthday, Ellen bought Jacob a brass watch. She had had the lid engraved:

> *I love you, Jacob,*
> *my old man forever.*
> *Ellen*

"I love you too, Ellen," said Jacob. "When you are a little older, we will be married, but we must wait a year or two more." He kissed her.

"One year!" she said, kissing him back. "Next year, we'll be wed!"

Jacob admired his fine watch.

"One year, then," he said with a smile.

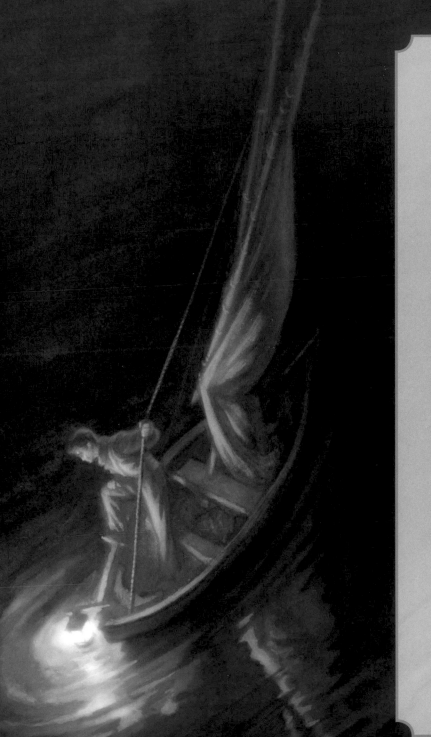

That evening, Jacob rowed his skiff in strong, swift strokes towards the church tower. He was about to throw his anchor over the side when he heard a sound.

It was muffled and distant, but it was a bell certainly.

A church bell.

Three chimes, then nothing but a numb echo across the lake. Jacob doubted his own senses. He leaned forwards and looked in the circle of light thrown by his lamp. Plenty of tiddlers, but no big fish. As his eyes got used to the darkness, he saw a strange glow moving between the dark shapes of the buildings in the depths of the lake. There was a sudden *thump!* His boat had drifted up against the clock tower.

Jacob shuddered. At the windows above, he saw a faint blue light.

"Who's there?" he called.

In a moment, he had tied up his boat and swiftly scaled the wall to the tall arched windows.

He jumped in and saw that there was no bell there. He looked down to where the stone steps should have disappeared into the lake water, but there was no water, only the faint blue glow.

As Jacob went down the steps, the light moved ahead ... just out of direct sight. Then he was at the bottom of the tower. It was damp, but there was no water and the door was slightly ajar. Beyond the door was the blue light.

How could that be?

He pushed the door open.

There was no flood, no torrent of water.

Before him was a young woman carrying a lamp.

"Who … ?" he tried to say. "What … ?" he spluttered as he staggered out of the tower.

He could not breathe … He could not walk … He could not stand.

Then there was only black.

When he awoke, Jacob was looking into the woman's face. She was pale and beautiful.

"No more of your spluttering!" she scolded him. "Eat this! Eat!"

She forced a cabbage-like weed into his mouth, and he swallowed it down.

"Come!" she ordered. "NOW!"

Jacob rose unsteadily to his feet, and she helped him along the church path, through the village he had known so well as a child. Ghostly faces peered at him from the windows. He heard them muttering and mumbling and mentioning his name.

"It's Jacob … Reuben and Celia's boy … Lilith has made a catch."

Soon a crowd shuffled behind them, and then a woman rushed out from one of the houses.

"Jacob ... my little Jacob ... why are you here?"

He and the woman stared at each other for a long moment, then she wrapped her cold arms around him and held him tight.

"Mother!"

"Jacob, you must leave here now!"

The young woman stepped between them.

"Enough of this!" she said, and the ghostly crowd pulled him along, away from his mother.

He thought he heard her calling, "Jacob! Get away! Don't eat ... our ... food! Get away, son!"

But the pale half-remembered faces were bearing down on him, asking him questions about their living kin, pinching his warm flesh!

And he was weak again... He couldn't breathe... He tried to push them away and then all was blackness.

When Jacob awoke again, he was on a bed in a fine house, and the young woman was spooning a kind of cabbage soup into his mouth. Jacob spluttered and pushed her away. She looked at him as if she was hurt.

"Eat the soup, Jacob! The soup is good!" she said. She made him eat it. And it was good. He felt its goodness running through him, making him strong, letting him breathe deeply.

The next morning, Reuben woke early. When he saw that Jacob wasn't asleep in his bed by the stove, he rushed out of the house.

"Jacob!" he shouted as he pulled the old rowing boat out of the shed.

"Jacob!" he screamed as he cast off into the lake.

"Jacob," he sobbed as his boat bumped the empty fishing skiff tied to the clock tower.

Later that day, Ellen sailed all around the lake, searching for Jacob. Others joined the search, but they found nothing. When they called off the search, there were mutterings about ghosts and evil and death in the haunted lake.

Ellen kept searching. After a week, she started fishing as she searched, and then she was just fishing.

She came to live with Jacob's father and slept in Jacob's bed by the stove.

Years passed and she worked with the old man, hauling, gutting, salting and smoking the fish, and once a week she took the small cart to the market below in the big town. Old Reuben took to sitting outdoors, winding ropes and bending hooks and staring across the lake.

Ellen grew from a girl into a woman. Her hard life showed on her face and on her rough hands and in her strong, muscled arms.

Below in sunken Spetzia, years did not go by. Days seemed to pass and weeks too, but not years. Time meant little there, but still Jacob looked at his watch often. He couldn't remember who had given it to him, and he couldn't clearly see the words engraved on the lid.

Sometimes he visited his mother, but she was always so sad and asked questions about his father that he could no longer remember the answers to.

He came to spend his days trailing along after Lilith, the beautiful young lady. He gazed into her pale grey eyes when she would let him. She would snap at him from time to time when she grew bored with him.

Jacob's life in the village was a strange kind of dream, and soon he could remember no other life.

One day Lilith said they were to be married.

She was beautiful, and he did remember wanting to be married.

"More cabbage, Jacob of the living? Eat up! EAT UP," she barked, and he was afraid … until she smiled her beguiling smile again.

One winter, most of the lake froze over, and on a bright afternoon Ellen was able to walk out to where the tower rose from the ice. She cleared some snow away and stared below.

As the winter sun faded, Ellen was sure she could see moving shapes and even lights below. She polished the ice with her cuff to see more clearly, and suddenly there was a flash of silver and two staring eyes in a pale face glaring at her.

Ellen leaped back, and the face was gone. There was a crack. The ice! She padded back the way she had come, but fissures were forming all around.

Her feet slipped in the slush. A slab of ice shifted under her weight, and she was in the freezing lake water. She tried to pull herself up, but she couldn't grip the wet ice. She was so cold now, and her clothes were so heavy. She was slipping under. But then, two strong hands grasped Ellen's arms.

"I've got you, lass," croaked old Reuben as he
dragged her from the water. He hoisted her into the boat,
then rowed between the ice floes to the shore as fast as he
could go.

"You have to leave this dead place, lass. There's
nothing for you here," said the old man as Ellen steamed
in front of the roaring stove.

"I could never leave Jacob," she answered. "No more
than you could leave Celia."

Lilith summoned Jacob.

"It's time we were married," she said. "You love me, don't you?" Silence.

She stamped her foot. "Of course you do!"

"Yes, I–I think so," Jacob stammered.

"You think so!" she screeched at him. She calmed herself immediately, and Jacob was lost in the stare of her beautiful grey eyes. Her cold hand touched his chin.

"We need you here, Jacob of the living... You remind us of ourselves ... our old selves.

"Once we are married, you and I can never be parted.

"You would never leave me, would you?"

"Never leave..." echoed Jacob.

"You're not secretly in love with some old hag of a fish-wife, are you?" she said icily.

"Not in love..." said Jacob.

"Then we'll be married tomorrow!"

"Tomorrow."

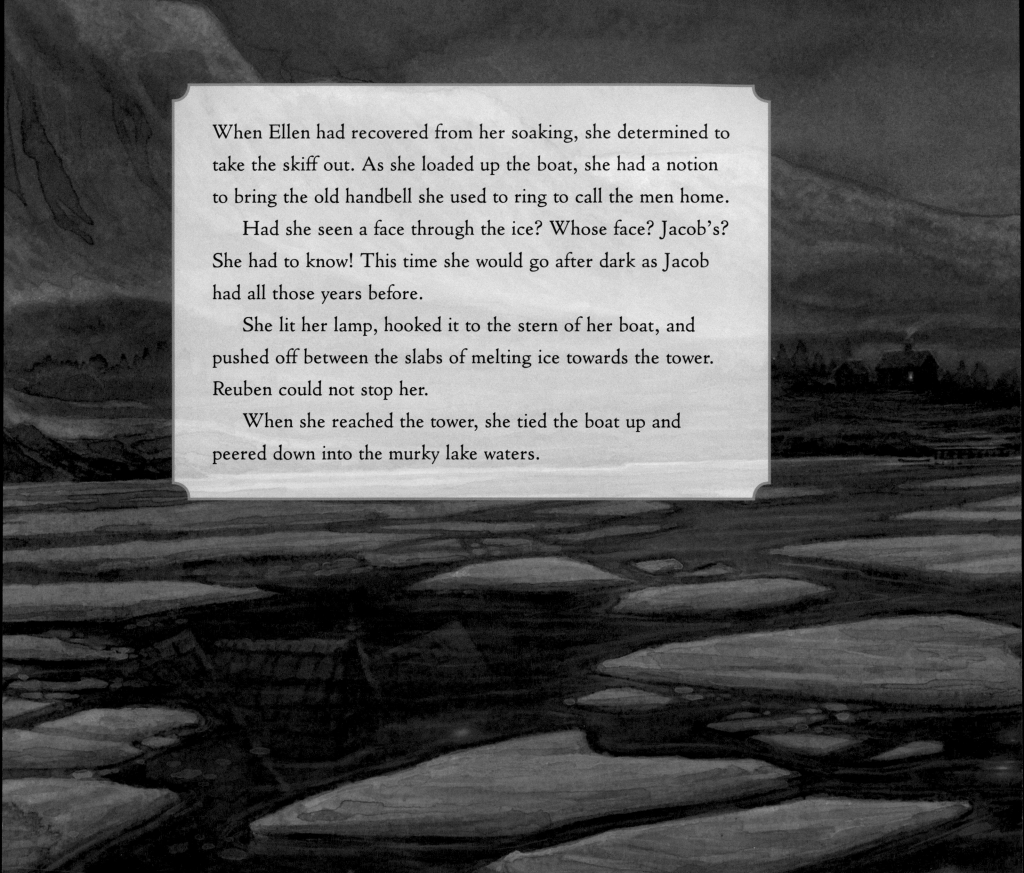

When Ellen had recovered from her soaking, she determined to take the skiff out. As she loaded up the boat, she had a notion to bring the old handbell she used to ring to call the men home.

Had she seen a face through the ice? Whose face? Jacob's? She had to know! This time she would go after dark as Jacob had all those years before.

She lit her lamp, hooked it to the stern of her boat, and pushed off between the slabs of melting ice towards the tower. Reuben could not stop her.

When she reached the tower, she tied the boat up and peered down into the murky lake waters.

Jacob and his beautiful bride-to-be paraded through the village to the church.

His eye was drawn to the church tower. He was used to seeing the strange watery clouds that obscured the view of the upper part of the tower, but this evening, there was a dark shadow with an intense glow at one end floating there.

A thought jumped into his head: Catch a perch or two tonight, lass. *And he said it aloud to Lilith.*

"Catch a perch or two tonight, lass."

She looked horrified at him and then saw the shadow above them.

"No!" she screeched.

At that moment a bell rang in the tower. Not a ghostly distant chime but a clanging racket that penetrated the fog in Jacob's mind. He thought, This is not the one I love! *and he took a step away.*

"Jacob!" Lilith looked sternly at him. "Come back here!"

Jacob took another step away.

"Seize him!" Lilith screamed, and the ghostly neighbours moved to stop Jacob, but he was off now and running. Lilith blocked the door to the church tower, and he dodged away as the ghosts bore down on him.

In the belfry, Ellen rang and rang the handbell, and when she stopped, her ears hummed in the silence. She was embarrassed by the din she had made.

You fool, Ellen. Jacob's been dead these fifteen years. He's never coming home again, she thought. She clambered back down to her skiff and sailed away.

Jacob eluded the ghosts, but he was tiring. The shadow and its light were sailing away! He picked up a stone and threw it toward the keel up above. No good. The ghosts were coming at him from all sides now. He slung another stone at the shadow above. Another miss.

Cold bony fingers caught him and held him tight. Jacob was weak and coughing now. He could not escape.

"Come, Jacob, your bride is waiting!" said one of his captors.

The shadow and its light were far away now ... almost gone.

Jacob managed to squeeze a hand into his pocket and pull out his watch. He studied it hard. Just then Celia burst through the group and shouted, "Let my son go!"

Jacob's eyes met his mother's for a moment, and then with a great heave, he broke free.

One last throw.

He hurled his watch with all his might.

Ellen was steering the skiff towards the lights of Reuben's house when she heard a splash, and something shiny jumped from the water onto the deck of the boat.

A fish?

No ... it was hard and round ... a watch!

She picked it up, and a shiver ran through her. She pried open the lid.

> *I love you, Jacob,*
> *my old man forever.*
> *Ellen.*

Jacob's watch!

She did not think... She could not understand ... but leaned on her rudder and turned her boat back through the ice towards the tower.

Where Jacob? Where? she thought.

She slung her stoutest ropes over the stern. She saw lights flashing below and shuddered with terror. Part of her wanted to sail away as fast as she could, but she stayed, drifting towards the ancient stones of the tower.

Suddenly her rope went taut as if she had caught the biggest fish.

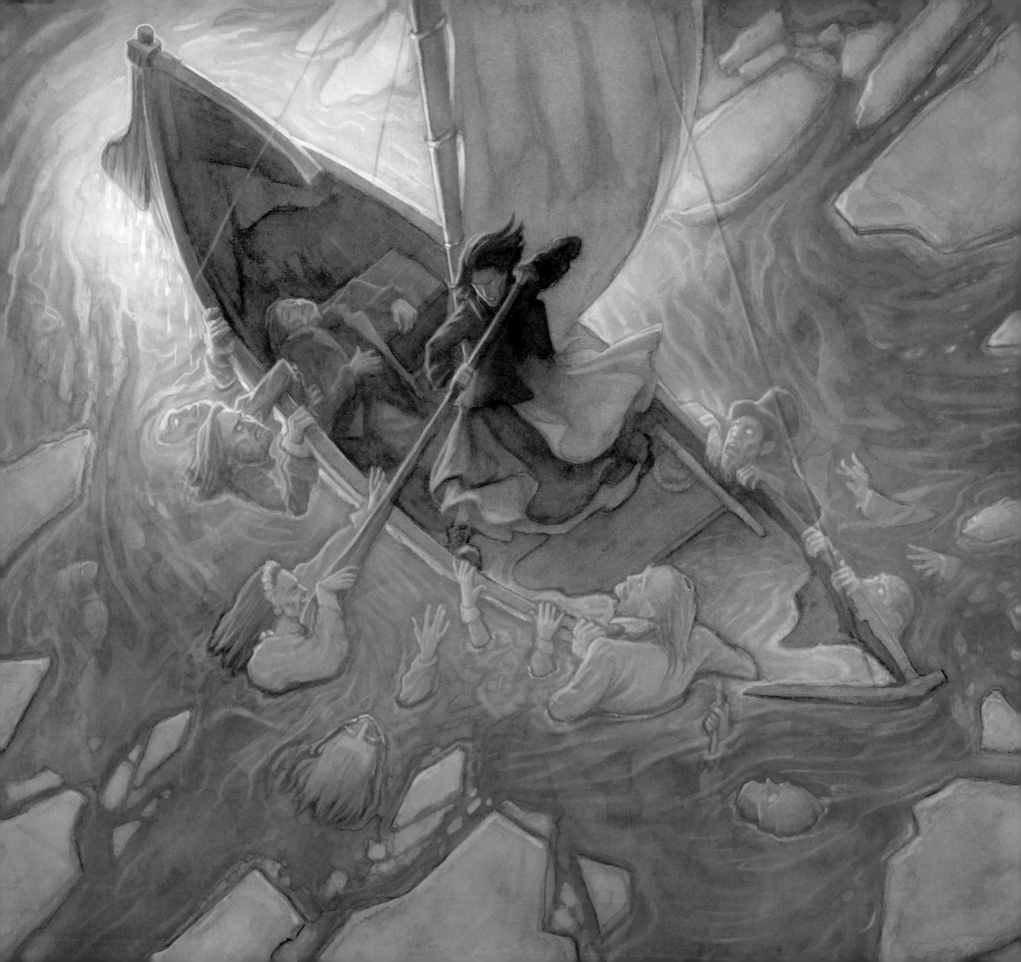

The bow of the skiff was in the water now.

The weight was too great.

She hauled on the rope till her fingers were raw, and then ... a hand!

A cold and ghostly white hand.

She pulled with all her might and up came an arm and a head and suddenly a young man was gasping on the deck of her boat. Jacob! More hands, cadaverous hands, were clawing to pull him back.

"No!" screamed Ellen as she kicked and whacked and jabbed at them with her oar. "He's mine!"

A sudden breeze caught the sail and whipped the skiff away, leaving the sunken village behind them.

Ellen looked at the form of the young man. Her young man, unchanged since the last time she saw him all those years before. Not gasping now. He was still.

She leaned over him and touched his cheek.

She kissed the cold face. She kissed his lips. Breathed life into him, and Jacob spluttered and coughed and looked up at her.

"Ellen? Is it you?" he gasped.

"Yes, it's me," she said through her tears.

"How long have I been gone?" He touched her face.

"Fifteen long years."

"Ellen, more beautiful now than ever. Always my girl!"

"My old man forever." They kissed again.

When they reached the shore, Jacob's father clutched his son tightly and wept.

They packed up all they had, then left at first light.

They went far away over the mountains to the coast, and as they travelled, Jacob told them his story ... about Lilith and about Celia.

Jacob and Ellen got married and fished together until she had to stop when the first baby came. Reuben sat by the shore winding ropes, bending hooks, and watching his grandchildren playing.

EPILOGUE

One day, when Jacob and Ellen and the children had gone to market, old Reuben took some bread and cheese and wine and loaded the rowing boat onto the small cart, along with a rope ladder he had made.

He left a goodbye note on the table and set off on the long journey back to Spetzia, back to the haunted lake.

For Evie and Barbara,
thank you for all your brilliant ideas
and for your enthusiasm through
the creation of this book.

Thanks also to Hilary Van Dusen, Lisa Rudden, and
everyone at Candlewick Press for your guidance and patience.

My special thanks to Ben and Sam Lynch, Bairbre Ni Chaoimh, Ashleigh
Dorrell, Jamie O'Neill, Clare Conville, Allison De Frees and Yve Williams.

First published 2020 by Walker Books Ltd
87 Vauxhall Walk, London SE11 5HJ

2 4 6 8 10 9 7 5 3 1

© 2020 P.J. Lynch

The right of P.J. Lynch to be identified as the author/illustrator of this work has been asserted by him
in accordance with the Copyright, Designs and Patents Act 1988

This book has been typeset in Cloister

Printed in China

British Library Cataloguing in Publication Data:
a catalogue record for this book is available from the British Library

ISBN 978-1-4063-9556-3

www.walker.co.uk